MY SPAGHETTI IS READY

50 things My Mama Would Say

ADRIAN WHITE

Copyright © 2021 by Adrian White

All rights reserved. No part of this book may be used or reproduced by any means, graphic, electronic, or mechanical, including photocopying, recording, taping, or by any information storage retrieval system, without the written permission of the publisher except in the case of brief quotations embodied in critical articles and reviews.

My Spaghetti is Ready is a book birthed from the things my mama would say to me, in the form of parables and stories to inspire, confuse and correct me. At that time, I believed them to be stuff that older people said to make you think they were crazy, but as I grew older, I began to know them as sayings to live, learn and love by. A book of translation and lessons learned while navigating this thing called life, so as you read and explore the sayings, I invite you to search yourself and remember some of the words your mama would say to you. Be inspired, engaged, captivated, and laugh out loud at the compilations. Some you may have heard, and others may be new but at least you have the memories of things my mama would say.

Mama would say #1

"My spaghetti is ready!"

Translation

When I was a child, I would watch my mom cook. One day she was making her delicious spaghetti and I wondered how she knew when her spaghetti was ready. I wanted to know because I was hungry and my tongue anticipated the taste! HaHa! So, I asked my mama: "Mama, how do you know your spaghetti is ready?" My mom said nothing but she grabbed a spoon, put it in the pot and pulled out a string of spaghetti and tossed the string on the wall. The string stuck to the wall and didn't move. I looked at her strangely, and she looked at me and said, "my spaghetti is ready when it sticks to the wall!"

Lesson Learned

If your spaghetti doesn't stick to the wall, boil the spaghetti a bit longer. *#cooking101*

Mama Would Say #2

"Do I look like a donut with a hole in my head?"

Translation

Don't tell me no lie because I can see right through the lie! I would try and think of a story to tell my mama when I did something I was not supposed to do but it never worked because she had been there and done that!

Lesson Learned

There is nothing new under the sun and mama knew a "fib" when she heard one, from experience!

Mama Would Say #3

"If I were you, I wouldn't wear that!"

Translation

Your outfit is inappropriate to leave this house!

Lesson Learned

If you have an outfit you want to wear, wait until mama is sleeping to leave the house...no that is not it! Here is the lesson learned - Always present yourself in a manner that exudes respect and do not think about representing me looking any other way.

Mama Would Say #4

"See a fool bump their head!"

Translation

People will misuse you
if you are not careful to discern their intentions!

Lesson Learned

Be very careful and watchful when allowing others into
your life-space and exist because people will take
advantage of you if you allow them to.

Mama would say #5

*"They put their pants
on one leg at a time just like you do!"*

Translation

Nobody is better than the other. God made us all the
same and everybody have problems and hang-ups
about themselves, but we are all equal.

Lesson Learned

You are just as important as anyone else.
Adrian, you matter (Insert your name here).

Mama would say #6

"If they dig one ditch, they better dig two!"

Translation

Don't come for mama unless she sends for you!

Lesson Learned

Don't mess with me, okay, *#period*

Mama would say #7

*"The same people you meet going up are
the same people you meet going down!"*

Translation

(I am still confused, so here is my translation.)
You get to heaven and think you're going in but
eventually, you go to hell! (shrug shoulders here)

Lesson Learned

Don't read so far into mama's sayings.

#LOL

Your space to translate here.

Mama would say #8

"You eat to live, not live to eat Adrian!"

Translation

Stop being greedy, my child.
Just eat enough to sustain you and not make you sick.

Lesson Learned

I was eating the poor woman
out of a house and a home.

#juststopitgirl

Mama would say #9

"Once you cook the beans, you can't replant them!"

Translation

Let go of mistakes you can't change.
What's done is done so move on and start fresh.

Lesson Learned

(Now I want some red beans and rice.)

#greedy #stayfocusedgirl

Mama would say #10

"You are not a product of your environment!"

Translation

If the environment you are in is not conducive for
growth and success, strive for more and achieve better.

Lesson Learned

The neighborhood or environment where I grew up
did not predicate who I am or what
I have accomplished.

Mama would say #11

"Kill them with kindness Adrian!"

Translation

The way you treat
others will teach them how to treat you.

Lesson Learned

My actions will create a blueprint
that others will follow to treat me.

#respect

Mama would say #12

"You're smelling yourself!

Translation

Fix your attitude young lady, before I fix it for you.

Lesson Learned

I needed to bathe my attitude and get
my emotions in check before mama put hands on me!

#thatladydontplay

Mama would say #13

"God will Bless an honest desire!"

Translation

God will discern the thoughts and intents of your heart. I would draw my mama pictures of houses and tell her, "mama one day, I will buy you a house. Mama would kiss my forehead and say to me,
"God will bless your desire."

Lesson Learned

God is blesses you when you bless others.

Mama would say #14

*"Do it right the first time and
you won't have to do it all over again!"*

Translation

Give me the best
you have to offer the first time or do it all over.

Lesson Learned

My mama will make a believer out of me! LOL! I
washed a cast iron skillet 10 times one night. *#huh
#iwastired #mamadidntcare #skilletneverbeensoclean*

Mama would say #15

"I mean what I said, and I said what I mean!"

Translation

I gave my answer, so don't you ask me again
or say anything else about it.

Lesson Learned

It is finished! I dare you to ask mama again!

#2blessed2bestressed
#leavemamaalone

Mama would say #16

"An empty wagon makes a lot of noise!"

Translation

Shh! Sit down, read and gain some knowledge.
That way you will be quiet and can learn.

Lesson Learned

I was making too much noise for mama.

#girlsitdownsomewhere
#mamacantstandallthatnoise

Mama would say #17

"It's about to be a whooping spree!"

Translation

Mama whooping everybody in the place.

Lesson Learned

Pray!

#help
#Jesusbeafence

Mama would say #18

"I'm going to be on you like white on rice!"

Translation

You about to get these hands
laid on you and not for prayer.

Lesson Learned

Mama had anger issues!

#getacounsler
#ifieverneededthelorditsnow

Mama would say #19

"Act your age, not your shoe size!"

Translation

You are too old to be doing childish things,
grow-up please!

Lesson Learned

Don't stay in the same place
you were at ten and you're now seventeen.

#why

<hr>

Mama would say #20

<hr>

"Children are to be seen and not heard!"

Translation

Girl if you don't sit your lil tail down and shut up!

Lesson Learned

Wait until I'm grown to speak!

#LOL
#nowitalkalot

Mama would say #21

"Ha!Ha!it's up to you! Just like the caller told Adrian!"

Translation

Whatever you choose, make sure it's your decision. One day I answered the telephone and the caller laugh and said, "it's up to you!" My mom asked me what the caller said and I told her and in turn, she continues to spew this phrase as a declaration in decision making and a life lesson.

Lesson Learned

Next time don't answer the phone!

#Why

Mama Would say #22

"I will knock you into the middle of next week!"

Translation

Don't try me Boo! Boo!
Because this ain't what you want!

#forreal

Lesson Learned

Mama needed a therapist!

#angerissues
#rotflmbo
#iwasafraid

Mama would say #23

"Y'all kids be quiet!
I need to hear a rat piss on cotton!"

Translation

I need some peace and quiet time!

Lesson Learned

Can you hear a rat piss on cotton?

#ooomama
#loading
#istilldontknow
#confused

Mama would say #24

"People will talk about you and they don't have
a pot to piss in or a window to pour it out!"

Translation

Don't worry about what people say about
you because they are miserable! Keep going!

Lesson Learned

Don't worry about what folk says about you!

#miserylovescompany
#yougogirl

Mama would say #25

*"When we get here if anyone asks you if you're hungry
and you're not, say no and even if you are hungry,
say NO!"*

Translation

If you get here and embarrass me like
I don't feed you, I will be to see you!

Lesson Learned

Do what mama say and you won't be hurt!

#makemecatchacase
#idareyou

Mama would say #26

*"Get out of here devil, you don't live here
and you are not allowed here!"*

Translation

Satan the lord rebuke you, loose here in Jesus name!

Lesson Learned

I have a praying mother and she ain't afraid
to activate the power of God!

#peace

Mama would say #27

"Well, ain't this a blip!"

Translation

This some bull! This don't make no sense!

Lesson learned

What is a Blip?

#huh #50yearsstilldontknow #ohwell

Mama would say #28

"Well, ain't that the pot calling the kettle black!"

Translation

How are you talking about someone
and you ain't no better!

Lesson Learned

Stop talking about people and try to help.

#whoareyou

Mama would say #29

"Be yourself and don't be nobody else!"

Translation

Be the best you!

Lesson learned

Can't nobody beat you being you.

Mama would say # 30

"Honor your mother and live!"

Translation

Respect mama!

Lesson learned

If I want to live, I better be respectful to mama.

Mama would say #31

*"Beat your head upside the wall
and say dummy, dummy, dummy!"*

Translation

What you did was not smart
and you should feel bad! So don't do it again!

Lesson Learned

Sometimes life's choices are a hard pill to swallow and
the choices you make will affect you dearly.

Mama would say #32

"You want your sippy cup?"

Translation

You're being childish and you need to stop!

Lesson Learned

When life comes at you, be ready to react like an adult.

#juststepawayfromthesippycup

*"On Christ the solid rock I stand,
all other ground is sinking sand!"*

Translation

God is mama everything.

Lesson Learned

If I can depend on anyone, I can depend on God.

#haveyoutriedhim

Mama would say #34

*"If you want to shorten your days on earth,
then disrespect mama!"*

Translation

I was scared when she said this to me!

#pleaselord

Lesson Learned

I want to live out the days that God promised me
so I will be good to my mama.

#Live
#please

Mama would say #35

"Give credit where credit is due!"

Translation

Encourage and uplift others
when they have performed well.

Lesson Learned

It's a blessing to honor others.

Mama would say #36

"I brought you in this world and I'll take you out!"

Translation

Don't do it! Don't try me!

Lesson Learned

Mama please, don't kill me!

#sleptwithoneeyeopen
#pleasetouchhermindlord
#ibelievedher

Mama would say #37

"Don't cut off your nose to spite your face!"

Translation

Stop doing things that don't make any sense!

Lesson Learned

Stay away from knives and sharp objects!

#ineedmynose

"You're funky than a jay bird!"

Translation

Your behind stank! LOL

Lesson Learned

Go wash your behind!

#un
#yousmellittoo
#bye

Mama would say #39

"You don't know Sh—from Shinola!"

Translation

Shut up because you don't know a doggone thing!

Lesson Learned

Do my research before coming for mama!

#tooyoungtoknow
#getittogether
#milkbehindyourears

Mama would say #40

"A hard head makes a soft behind!"

Translation

You're going to have to sleep on your stomach after I spank your butt for doing what I told you not to do!

Lesson Learned

Do squats and increase muscle mass
in my glutes for reinforcement.

#makegoodchoices
#ouch

Mama would say #41

"You still a rookie, wet behind the ears!"

Translation

You can never tell me nothing as young as you are.

Lesson Learned

Don't tell mama nothing, okay!

Mama would say #42

"Hold your horses and turn your wagon around!"

Translation

Slow down!

Lesson Learned

You're doing too much, so just stop and regroup.

#toomuchnoise

Mama would say #43

"The Bigger they are, the harder they fall!"

Translation

Don't be afraid of nobody.

Lesson learned

Whatever I do, don't let anyone overpower me.

#davidandgoliath

Mama would say #44

"The more I teach you, the dumber I get!"

Translation

I don't know how to do this fifth-grade math and every time I try to teach you, I just don't know what to do!

Lesson Learned

It's better to use the expertise of a math tutor.

#hahahaha
#whoinventedthismath
#askyourteachernotme

"As for me and my house, we will serve the lord!"

Translation

Jesus is the reason for everything,
so get up and get ready for church!

Lesson Learned

I know the dates for church service and how long we
would be in church, so deal with it. (shrug shoulders)

#ilovejesus
#jesuslovesme

Mama would say #46

"Why you looking like who did it and what for!"

Translation

Child what you got on?

Lesson Learned

Don't think you sharp because
mama will bring you down a bunch of levels.

#youshollisugly
#noyoudidnt
#childplease

"Use your head for more than a hat rack!"

Translation

Think before you speak or act!

Lesson Learned

I have one brain, so use it responsibly.

#isthisthingon

Mama would say #48

"I'll knock you two buttonholes lower!"

Translation

I wish you would! You don't know me by now child?"

Lesson Learned

Mama likes to fight and she would fight kids too!

#toofunny
#yallhelp
#callthepeople

Mama would say #49

"The devil is a liar!"

Translation

The devil is a lie!

Lesson Learned

The devil is a lie!

#noothertranslationneeded

Mama would say #50

"You have a right to your opinion!"

Translation

Say what you want about the subject, that's on you.

Lesson Learned

Your opinion is simply that, your opinion.

#theend

www.ingramcontent.com/pod-product-compliance
Lightning Source LLC
Chambersburg PA
CBHW060943130726

48001CB00003B/1041